SHAKE UP
SCIENCE 2

Pearson Education Limited
Edinburgh Gate
Harlow
Essex CM20 2JE
England
and Associated Companies throughout the world.

www.pearsonelt.com

© Pearson Education Limited 2016

All rights reserved; no part of this publication may be reproduced, stored in a retrieval system, or transmitted in any form or by any means, electronic, mechanical, photocopying, recording, or otherwise without the prior written permission of the Publishers.

First published 2016
ISBN: 978-1-2921-4474-0

Set in ArtaStd, BradleyHandITCStd, FuturaLTPro, GillSansInfantStd, ITCAvantGardeStd, LubalinGraphStd, MemphisSRPro, MorrisFreestyleStd, SpartanLTStd, VAGRoundedLTPro, ZapfDingbatsStd, ZemkeHandITCStd
ARP Impression 98

Printed in Great Britain by Ashford Colour Press Ltd., Gosport

Authorized Adaptation from the U.S. English Language Edition, entitled Interactive Science, Copyright © 2012 by Pearson Education, Inc. or its affiliates. Used by permission. All Rights Reserved.

Pearson and Scott Foresman are trademarks, in the US and/or other countries, of Pearson Education, Inc. or its affiliates.

This publication is protected by copyright, and prior to any prohibited reproduction, storage in a retrieval system, or transmission by any for or by any means, electronic, mechanical, photocopying, recording or likewise, permission should be obtained from International Rights Sales, 221 River Street, Hoboken, NJ 07030 U.S.A

This book is authorized for sale worldwide.

Acknowledgements
Picture credits
The publisher would like to thank the following for their kind permission to reproduce their photographs:

(Key: b-bottom; c-centre; l-left; r-right; t-top)

123RF.com: Alinamd 38/2, Astragal 69/1, Andi Berger 34/1, Serge Bertasius 22 (b), Sergiy Bykhunenko 32/1 (right), Paulo Cruz 72/1, 83 (unit 9), Maksym Darakchi 38/3, 83 (unit 5), greggr 56/1, Ivan Gulei 12/2, Jennifer Huls 56b, Jules_Kitano 72/2, Madllen 58cr, Janunya Napapong 72b/3, Boris Ryzhkov 30/6, Sborisov 12/1, 29tr, Anton Starikov 8/1, Hannu Viitanen 68/2, Valentyn Volkov 58r, Maria Wachala 12b, Ivonne Wierink 33, Sybille Yates 38/4, 39/2; **Alamy Images:** Foodcollection 28/8, 86t, Jeremy Pardoe 10/5, 11b; **Fotolia.com:** Bit24 30/5, Vladyslav Danilin 39/4, Freshidea 58tr, Warren Goldswain 36/3, Gorilla 36/4, Eric Isselée 17b, Gregory Johnston 14 (air), 14/5, Lanych 58tl, Iarcobasso 30/1, MarFot 10/4 (clothes), Nik Merkulov 10/4 (wood), mettus 36/1, MNStudio 36/2, Monkey Business 25, Popova Olga 8/5, ptasha 69/2, Kimberly Reinick 35/3, Rixie 8/4, 39/3, Mauro Rodrigues 40/1, Gordana Sermek 10/4 (clothes), Svphilon 44/3, TuTheLens 86b, Weerapat1003 14/3; **Getty Images:** De Agostini Picture Library 39/1, Hero Images 9, KenCanning 10/1, 11t, Klaus Nigge 19, The Image Bank 76b, Universal Images Group 44/4; **Imagemore Co., Ltd:** 4/1, 5 (stapler), 28/1; **Pearson Education Ltd:** Gareth Boden 70b, Lisa Payne Photography 77c, 85b, 87b; **Shutterstock.com:** 58cl, 75/4, Apdesign 72b/2, Artmim 8/3, Aztekphoto 28/6, B747 48/3, Andrey N Bannov 16/3, Andrey Bayda 66t, Bikeriderlondon 42/2, Barry Blackburn 50/2, BlueOrange Studio 45tl, 45tr, Natalia Bratslavsky 28/2, Simon Bratt 72b/4, Danette Carnahan 17/3, Chbaum 43tc, Hung Chung Chih 32/4, Robert Cicchetti 48/4, cyo bo 20/1, 29bl, James DeBoer 83 (unit 3), Serg Dibrova 69/3, Digital Media Pro 77/2, Eaglesky 14 (soil), 14/2, Elena Elisseeva 64 (plane), ErickN 66b, Konstantin Faraktinov 64 (oil), 65bl, Fotofermer 30/3, Fremme 38/6, Gelpi JM 70/2, Pashin Georgiy 20/2, Eric Gevaert 21, Monika Gniot 72/3, Warren Goldswain 78t, Johanna Goodyear 56/2, Nicole Gordine 62tl, gorillaimages 32/2, Jiang Hongyan 64 (iron), Horiyan 8/2, Hurst Photo 64 (fan), Hxdbzxy 32/3, 34/3, 35/2, Maxim Ibragimov 67tr, Ilike 5t, Imagedb.com 67tl, Irena13 63t, Eric Isselee 20/5, Ivancovlad 4/2, 5 (hammer), 28/3, Marcel Jancovic 76/3, Nick Jay 68/4, Joel_420 50/3, Dmitry Kalinovsky 20/6, kavram 48/1, Levent Konuk 22/5, Lev Kropotov 64 (charcoal), 83 (unit 8), Kzww 4/3, 5 (screwdriver), 28/9, Daniel Leppens 74/4, 75/3, 81cr, LiAndStudio 26tr, 29cl, Dmitriev Lidiya 47, Lizard 43tl, Anatoliy Lukich 22/2, 22cr, Andrew Lundquist 76/2, Mangostock 37, MartinMaritz 18/1, 86c, V. J. Matthew 26tl, Oleg Mikhaylov 77/3, Monkey Business Images 34/4, Monticello 56/3, n_eri 68/3, 69b, Namning 56/5, Oleg Nekhaev 22/3, nikkytok 14 (water), 14/1, 74/2, 75/1, Norbert1986 13t, Sergey Novikov 78b, Anita Patterson Peppers 68/6, Pavel L Photo and Video 83 (unit 6), Sean Pavone 74/3, Pchais 40/4, 87tl, Phant 8/6, PHB.cz (Richard Semik) 75/2, 76/4, Loo Joo Pheng 22/4, 22cl, Phofotos 68/1, 70/4, pio3 70/3, 81cl, pjcross 68b, 69/4, Plavevski 20/4, Lee Prince 42/1, 43tr, Quaoar 38/5, Racorn 10/6, 83 (unit 1), Alexander Raths 7/1, 7/2, 7/3, Tom Reichner 16/1, 17/2, 22/1, 83 (unit 2), Rohappy 76/1, 81b, Martina Roth 40/3, Sakkmesterke 30/4, 83 (unit 4), samarttiw 44/2, Ruslan Semichev 62tc, Zvyagintsev Sergey 4/4, 5 (scissors), 28/4, Marcio Jose Bastos Silva 74/1, Sinelyov 20/3, 29br, Smereka 28/5, Smit 44/1, Kent Sorensen 22 (a), Lori Sparkia 62tr, srekap 22 (c), Sergio Stakhnyk 50/1, Florin Stana 77b, Minerva Studio 48/2, 49, Sunsinger 17/1, Tania A 38/1, 65tl, Charles Taylor 87c, Winai Tepsuttinun 56/4, Kenny Tong 12/3, TonLammerts 63c, 83 (unit 7), Triff 14 (light), 14/4, 64 (sun), Suzanne Tucker 35/1, Rudy Umans 18/2, UMB-O 68/5, Martin Valigursky 77/1, Eva Vargyasi 70/1, Vitalinka 34/2, VVO 40/2, 87tr, wavebreakmedia 6, 15, 31, WDG Photo 79, withGod 22/6, Jolanta Wojcicka 18/3, Worldpics 13b, 84, Gayvoronskaya Yana 30/2, Feng Yu 4/5, 5 (nails), 10/4 (nails), 28/7, 58l, Peter Zijlstra 16/2, zukerka 72b/1

All other images © Pearson Education

Cover photo © Front: **Getty Images:** monkeybusinessimages r; **Shutterstock.com:** S. Kuelcue l; Back: **Shutterstock.com:** Ozerov Alexander c, hin255 l, Sergey Novikov r

Contents

Unit 1 — **The Design Process** 4
How do you solve problems?

Unit 2 — **Living Things and Their Environments** 12
What do plants and animals need?

Unit 3 — **Plants and Animals** 20
How are living things alike and different?

Review 1–3 28

Unit 4 — **Body and Health** 30
What do I need to be healthy?

Unit 5 — **Earth and Sky** 38
What can you say about Earth and sky?

Unit 6 — **Weather** 46
How can you describe weather?

Review 4–6 54

Unit 7 — **Matter** 56
How can you describe matter?

Unit 8 — **Energy** 64
What can energy do?

Unit 9 — **Movement** 72
How can you describe ways objects move?

Review 7–9 80

Skills 82

Unit 1 The Design Process

How do you solve problems?

1 What are the tools? Look and write.

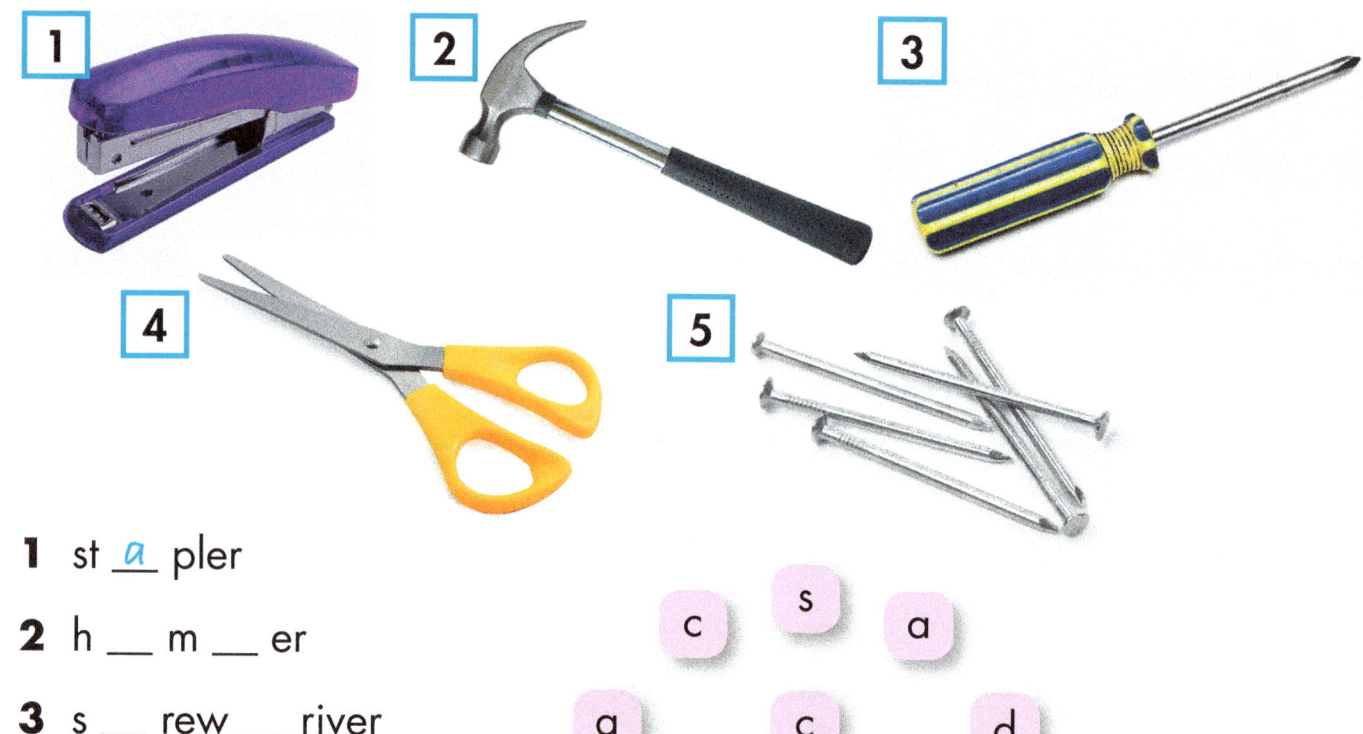

1 st _a_ pler

2 h __ m __ er

3 s __ rew __ river

4 s __ is __ ors

5 n __ __ ls

2 Where do you use these tools? Read and circle.

1 hammer   at home / at school

2 screwdriver   at home / at school

3 stapler   at home / at school

4 scissors   at home / at school

5 nails   at home / at school

③ **Making a birdhouse. What tools do you need? Look at 1, think, and write.**

_____

> **Reading Tip**
>
> Look online for information. A website can tell you what tools you need.

④ **Check your answer to 3. Read and mark (✓).**

Dad: Do we have all the tools we need?

Tom: We have the hammer.

Dad: Where are the nails?

Tom: They're here.

Dad: Now, where is the screwdriver?

Tom: Here it is!

Make a Birdhouse

You need:

- a stapler ☐
- a hammer ✓
- some nails ☐
- some scissors ☐
- a screwdriver ☐

⑤ **What tools do you have? Draw and complete for you.**

At school, I have _____
_____
_____.

At home, _____
_____
_____.

Unit 1   5

Lesson 1 · What is technology?

1 Jack and technology. Read and write *yes* or *no*.

Jack likes science. He wants to be a scientist. Scientists use technology to make discoveries. Jack likes to use technology. His tablet is his favorite kind of technology. He wants to use technology to invent something or to make an important discovery.

1 Jack wants to be a scientist.   _yes_
2 Jack wants to be a teacher.   _____
3 Scientists use technology.   _____
4 Jack doesn't like technology.   _____
5 He likes his tablet.   _____

2 What goes together? Read and match the sentence halves.

1 He wants to be   a to make a discovery.
2 He wants to use technology   b kind of technology.
3 He likes to   c a scientist.
4 A tablet is a   d use technology.

3 Scientists. Look and write *is* or *are*.

Grammar Tip

This **is** a scientist. They **are** scientists.

1 He <u>is a scientist</u>_____.

2 She _____.

3 They _____.

4 What is your favorite kind of technology? Draw and complete for you. Choose from the words in the box.

| computer | tablet | cell phone | car | bicycle |

This is a _____.   This is a _____.

Unit 1 7

Lesson 2 • What are objects made of?

1 What materials are the objects made of? Read and circle.

1 The clock is made of (plastic) / wood.
2 The table is made of wood / rock.
3 The doll's clothes are made of plastic / cotton.
4 The bridge is made of rock / wood.
5 The socks are made of cotton / rock.
6 The pen is made of wood / plastic.

2 Read and circle *T* (true) or *F* (false).

1 Rock is natural.   (T)/ F
2 Cotton is soft.   T / F
3 Wood is natural.   T / F
4 Cotton is natural.   T / F
5 Rock is soft.   T / F

3 Natural and man-made materials. Read and write *yes* or *no*.

Reading Tip
Read the text carefully. Are the sentences correct?

I am in my science class. We are looking at natural and man-made materials. The tables are made of wood. It is a natural material. My chair is made of plastic. It is a man-made material. My clothes are made of cotton. My pencil is made of wood. Are they natural or man-made?

1 The tables are made of wood.   _yes_
2 It is a natural material.   _____
3 The chair is made of rock.   _____
4 Her clothes are made of cotton.   _____
5 Her pencil is made of plastic.   _____

4 What are the objects in **3** made of? Read and write.

1 The tables are made of ___wood___.
2 The chair is made of _____.
3 The clothes are made of _____.
4 The pencil is made of _____.

5 Think of an object. What is it made of? Draw and complete for you.

This is a _____.
It is made of _____.

Unit 1 **9**

Lesson 3 • What is the design process?

1 The design process. Look, read, and circle the words from the box.

> share   goal   solution   ~~problem~~
> materials   plan   labels   test

How do we solve a problem?

1 First, think of the (problem).

2 Next, decide on the goal and think of a solution.

3 Make a plan and draw. Use labels.

4 Choose your materials.

5 Make a test.

6 Record, write, and share.

2 Look at the poster in **1**. Read and circle.

1 What's the problem?
   a The birds don't like the plants.
   b The people don't like the plants.
   (c) The birds like eating the plants.

2 What's the goal?
   a Make a birdhouse.
   b Stop the birds eating the plants.
   c Give the birds food.

3 What's the solution?
   a Design and make a birdhouse.
   b Design and make some clothes.
   c Design and make a scarecrow.

3 Read and write. Use the verbs in parentheses.

1 First, ___make___ the body. (make)

2 Next, _____ the head. (make)

3 Next, _____ the nose, mouth, and eyes. (draw)

4 Next, _____ the scarecrow a scarf and hat. (give)

Grammar Tip

First, make a plan and draw.
Next, label the design.

4 Can you design a scarecrow? Make a plan and draw. Use labels.

wood   rocks   nails
tape   hat   scarf

Unit 1   11

Unit 2 Living Things and Their Environments

What do plants and animals need?

1 Different environments. Look and match.

a desert   **b** forest   **c** pasture

1

2

3

2 Where do sheep live? Look and write.

sheep

p _ _ _ _ _ _ _

3 Can you think of an environment? Draw and label:

1 the environment

2 an animal that lives in the environment

3 a plant that lives in the environment

4 Which animal? Look, read, and write.

Fact File: s _ _ _ _

Need: water, food, sunlight
Live: pasture
Eat: grass
Drink: water
Products: wool, meat, cheese, milk

5 Facts about sheep. Read and circle.

1 Sheep live in (a pasture) / the desert.

2 They eat **animals** / **grass**.

3 They drink **water** / **milk**.

4 We can get **milk** / **water** from sheep.

6 Facts about cows. Read and write.

| water | grass | milk | pasture | ~~sunlight~~ |

Fact File: cows

Need: water, _sunlight_, food
Live: _____
Eat: _____
Drink: _____
Product: _____

Unit 2 13

Lesson 1 · What do living things need?

1 What can you see? Look and match.

- a light
- b water
- c air
- d soil
- e nutrients

2 What do plants need? Read and think. Mark (✓) and write.

air ✓

water ☐

soil ☐

light ☐

Plants need a i r and w __ __ __.
They need l __ __ __ __ to make food. The s __ __ __ gives
them the n __ __ __ __ __ __ __ they need.

14 Unit 2

3 What do animals need? Read and mark (✓) five things.

Needs of animals

| air | ✓ | soil | ☐ | water | ☐ | cotton | ☐ |
| rocks | ☐ | shelter | ☐ | light | ☐ | food | ☐ |

4 What do people need? Read and write.

People need nutrients. Here are some people eating breakfast. There are some nutrients in the food and in the drinks. There is some orange juice and some milk to drink. There are some apples and there is some toast to eat. People need (1) _f_ _o_ _o_ _d_, (2) w __ __ __ r, (3) l __ __ __ t, space, (4) s __ __ __ __ __ r, and (5) a __ r.

5 Are the objects countable or uncountable? Read and circle.

1 There is / (There are) some people.
2 There is / There are some shelter.
3 There is / There are some light.
4 There is / There are some nutrients in the food.

Grammar Tip

There is some food.
There are some people.

6 What do you need? Complete for you.

air   water   light   food   soil   shelter

I need _____.
I don't need _____.

Lesson 2 · How do plants and animals live in land environments?

1 What can you see? Look, read, and match.

- [ ] **a** Lizards live in some deserts. Deserts are very dry. They get very little rain or snow.
- [1] **b** Black bears live in some forests. Forests have many trees and other plants.
- [ ] **c** Prairie dogs live in some prairies. Prairies are flat, and they have grass.

2 Read and circle *T* (true) or *F* (false).

1. An environment has food, water, and air.   **(T)** / F
2. Land has rocks, soil, and sky.   T / F
3. A forest is a water environment.   T / F
4. Deserts are very dry.   T / F
5. Plants grow in deserts.   T / F
6. Prairies are flat and have grass.   T / F

3 Can you name the environment? Read and write.

desert   ~~prairie~~   forest

1 These horses live on a flat land with a lot of grass. They live on the __prairie.__

2 This bear lives in an environment with a lot of trees. It lives in the _____.

3 This plant lives in a dry environment with very little rain or snow. It lives in the _____.

4 Read and write about lizards. Write *has* or *have*.

Lizards (**1**) __have__ four legs, and they (**2**) _____ big feet. Some lizards (**3**) _____ light-colored skin. This lizard is small, and it (**4**) _____ a fat tail. Its big feet are good for climbing trees.

Grammar Tip

A prairie **has** grass. Forests **have** many trees.

5 What's your favorite animal? Complete for you.

horse   black bear   prairie dog   lizard

My favorite animal is _____.
_____ lives _____.
It has _____.

Unit 2   17

Lesson 3 • How do plants and animals live in water environments?

1 Can you name the environment? Read and write.

| marsh   ocean   swamp   ~~wetland~~ |

1 A __wetland__ is an environment that is covered with water.

2 A _____ is a wetland that has grasses.

3 A _____ is a wetland that has soft, wet land and many trees.

4 An _____ is an environment with a lot of salty water.

2 Where do the animals live? Look and match.

1 heron   2 alligator   3 fish

a ocean   b swamp   c marsh

3 What helps the animals live in the environment? Read and write.

| gills   fins   ~~beaks~~   tails   legs |

1 Herons catch fish with their long, sharp __beaks__.

2 Herons have long, thin _____.

3 Alligators use their long, strong _____ to help them swim.

4 Fish use _____ to take in oxygen from the water.

5 Fish have _____ to help them swim.

4 What is a flamingo? Look and circle.

It's a plant / bird / fish.

> **Reading Tip**
> You can find the answer in the text.

Flamingos

Flamingos are birds that live in wetlands. They have very long legs. Their legs can be longer than their bodies. They live in very big groups. They are pink or orange. The food they eat makes them this color.

5 Flamingo facts. Look at 4 again. Read and choose.

1 Flamingos live in _b_.
   a rivers
   b wetlands
   c the ocean

2 They have __.
   a long legs and a long neck
   b short legs and a short neck
   c long legs and a short neck

3 They live __.
   a alone
   b in very big groups
   c in very small groups

4 They are __.
   a red or orange
   b pink or red
   c pink or orange

6 Find out about a wetland animal or plant. Complete the chart.

What's its name?	It's a _____.
Where does it live?	_____
What helps it live in a wetland?	_____

Unit 2   19

Unit 3 Plants and Animals

How are living things alike and different?

1 What animal is it? Look and write.

> kitten   cat   ~~panda bear~~
> dog   newborn panda   puppy

1 _panda bear_   2 _____   3 _____

4 _____   5 _____   6 _____

2 What can you see in the photos? Look at **1** and write.

	Cat	Kitten	Dog	Puppy	Panda Bear	Newborn Panda
Number of legs?						
Tail? yes/no						
Color?						

20   Unit 3

3 What can you see in the photo? Look and read. Write *yes* or *no*.

1 Are they kittens? ___no___

2 Are they orangutans? _____

3 Is the parent very different from its baby? _____

Reading Tip

Use the photo to help you understand the text.

4 Read and circle *T* (*true*) or *F* (*false*).

My favorite animal at the zoo is the orangutan. The baby orangutan is like the mother. They are the same shape and color. They both have a big mouth, two ears, two eyes, and a nose. But the baby orangutan is smaller than the mother. He does not have hair on his head.

Mother and baby orangutans

1 The mother and the baby are very different.   T /(F)

2 The mother and the baby have big mouths.   T / F

3 The mother orangutan is smaller than the baby.   T / F

4 The baby orangutan has hair on his head.   T / F

5 What's your favorite baby animal? Complete for you.

| baby   puppy   kitten   newborn panda   orangutan |

1 My favorite baby animal is _____.

2 It has _____.

3 It eats _____.

Unit 3   21

Lesson 1 · What are some groups of living things?

1 Living things. Look, read, and write.

1 Which animal has the same shape as the cat?   _4_

2 Which animals live in water?   ___

3 Which animals can fly?   ___

4 Which animals have claws?   ___

2 Compare the animals. Look, read, and circle.

1 They (are) / aren't both living things.

2 They both have / don't have claws and tails.

3 They both have / don't have fur.

4 They have / don't have feathers.

5 They are / aren't the same size.

6 They are / aren't the same color.

3 Plants. Match the sentences with the photos.

1 Some plants have cones.   _c_

2 Some plants do not have flowers or cones.   ___

3 Plants with flowers make seeds.   ___

4. Animal or plant? Complete the mind maps.

backbone   cone   feathers   fur
leaf   roots   scales   seed

feathers   _____   _____   _____

Parts of an Animal   **Parts of a Plant**

_____   _____   _____   _____

5. Read the chart. Write.

Animal Group	Backbone	Features
Mammals	✓	fur/hair
Birds	✓	feathers
Fish	✓	gills, fins, scales
Reptiles	✓	dry skin, scales
Amphibians	✓	smooth wet skin
Insects	✗	legs

Reading Tip

A chart can help us sort information.

1 __Birds__ have a backbone and feathers.

2 _____ don't have a backbone.

3 _____ have dry skin, scales, and a backbone.

4 _____ have fur or hair.

5 _____ have gills, scales, and fins.

6. Complete for you. Use words from 5.

I have _____.

I don't have _____.

Unit 3   23

Lesson 2 • How are living things like their parents?

1 Look, read, and circle the words from the box.

~~parents~~   shape   young   alike   different

(Parents) and their young can look alike. Plants and their young are usually the same shape but a different size.

2 Ducklings and ducks. Read the text. Mark how they are alike (✓) and different (✗).

Ducklings and Their Parents

A duckling is a baby duck. These are ducklings and their parents. They are alike, and they are different. Both ducks and ducklings have two wings, orange beaks and legs, and feet to swim. Ducklings are small, and ducks are big. Ducklings have yellow bodies. Ducks have white bodies.

	Ducklings and Ducks
Size	✗
Color of Body	
Color of Legs and Beak	
Number of Wings	

3 Label the duckling. Look and write.

beak   ~~wings~~
feet   legs

1. wings
2.
3.
4.

4 Parents and babies. Read and complete the mind map.

ten   size   two   ten   two   can't   two   ~~size~~   can   two

- big _size_
- ____ arms
- ____ walk and speak
- ____ fingers
- ____ legs

People → **Parents**, **Babies**

Babies:
- ____ legs
- ____ fingers
- ____ walk and speak
- small ____
- ____ arms

5 Compare parents and babies. Read and write *is*, *are*, *has*, or *have*.

1. A baby __has__ a small body.
2. Babies _____ small and parents are big.
3. Parents and babies both _____ two legs.
4. A baby _____ young.
5. A baby _____ very short hair.

Grammar Tip

Parents **are** big.
A baby **is** small.
Parents **have** big legs.
A baby **has** small legs.

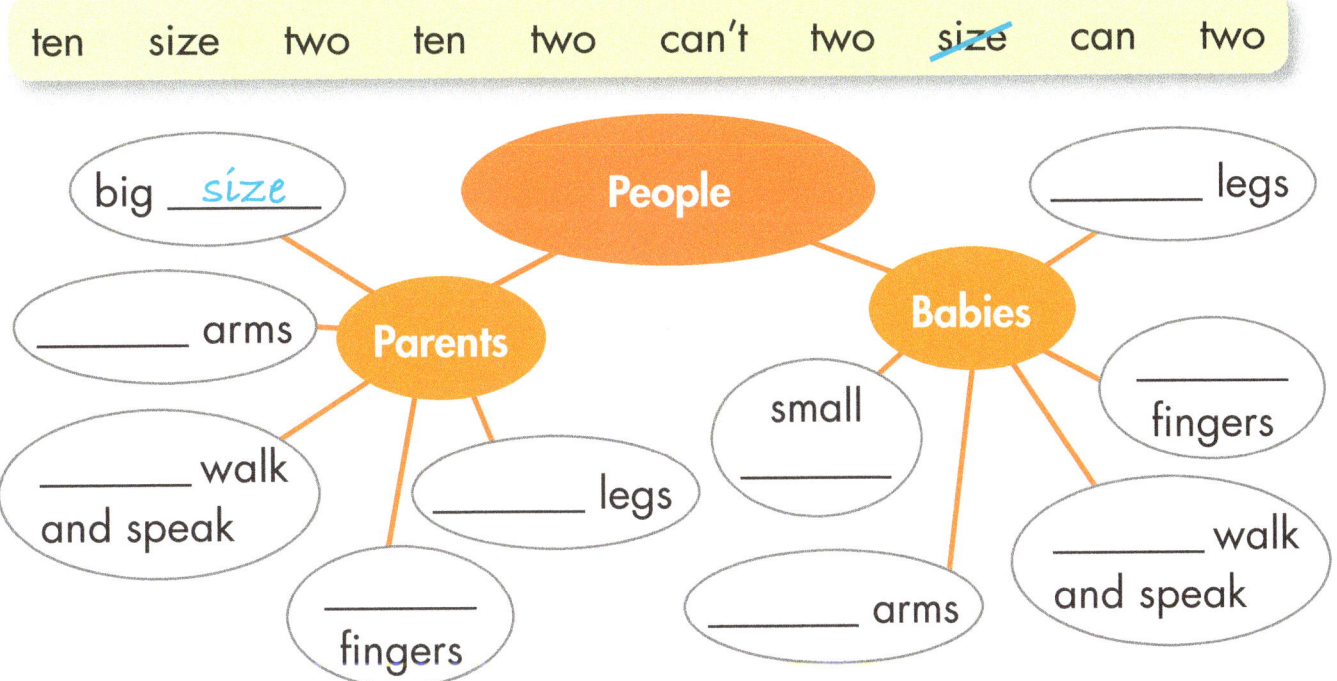

6 Can you describe you and your parents? Complete.

My parents are _____.
I am _____.
My parents have _____.
I have _____.

Unit 3   25

Lesson 3 · How are groups of living things different?

1 Alike and different. Circle in green how the petunias are alike. Circle in red how they are different.

Petunias

These are photos of petunias.
Petunias are a kind of plant.
All petunias have fuzzy, green leaves.
They can have different colored flowers.

2 What are zebras like? Read and label the picture.

~~black and white stripes~~   brown and white stripes
    herd   ears   tail

Zebras

Look at this herd of zebras. They have two small ears, four legs, and a tail. They have stripes, too. The baby zebra has brown and white stripes. The parents have black and white stripes. Zebras can hear very well, but they can't see the color orange. They eat plants, and they sleep on the grass. Zebras can run very fast.

1 black and white stripes
2 _____
3 _____
4 _____
5 _____

26   Unit 3

3 **What can zebras do? Look at 2. Read and circle *T* (true) or *F* (false).**

1 Zebras can see the color orange.   T /(F)
2 Zebras can sleep on the grass.   T / F
3 Zebras can run fast.   T / F
4 Zebras can't eat plants.   T / F
5 Zebras can hear very well.   T / F

4 **Look at 3. Read and write *can* or *can't* with the verb in parentheses.**

> **Grammar Tip**
>
> Zebras **can hear** very well.
> Zebras **can't see** orange.

1 Zebras __can run__ very fast. (run)
2 Zebras _____ orange. (see)
3 Zebras _____ plants. (eat)
4 Zebras _____ very well. (hear)

5 **What's your favorite animal? Draw and write.**

swim   fly   run   jump   hear   see

My favorite animal _____
_____.
It can _____
_____.
It can't _____
_____.

Unit 3   27

Review 1-3

1. **Look and circle the tools in red and the materials in blue.**

2. **Find the words in the wordsearch.**

1 stapler   2 hammer   3 scissors
4 nails   5 screwdriver 6 plastic
7 cotton   8 wood   9 rock

P	E	N	Y	K	S	S	D	W	G	P
L	S	O	L	X	K	C	X	O	C	E
S	T	A	P	L	E	R	E	O	H	S
C	H	A	R	N	V	E	T	D	A	C
A	Z	A	O	A	A	W	D	U	M	I
V	R	U	C	I	L	D	U	C	M	S
E	D	P	K	L	W	R	X	O	E	S
V	P	L	A	S	T	I	C	T	R	O
P	P	G	V	I	T	V	B	T	F	R
T	A	Y	J	S	B	E	V	O	D	S
I	N	M	A	U	M	R	P	N	S	H

28 Review 1-3

3 **Circle the odd one out.**

1 wetland   marsh   swamp   ocean   (shelter)
2 bear   mammal   reptile   amphibian   insect
3 air   nutrients   environment   water   light
4 wood   cotton   desert   rock   plastic
5 beak   tail   gills   fins   parent

4 **What can you remember? Do the quiz. Circle a, b, or c.**

1 Technology uses science to _____.
  a cut
  (b) help solve problems
  c cook

2 Plants need _____.
  a air, water, nutrients, and light
  b air and light
  c water and light

3 Plants can get nutrients from _____.
  a the light
  b the air
  c the soil

4 A forest has _____.
  a a prairie
  b many trees
  c deserts

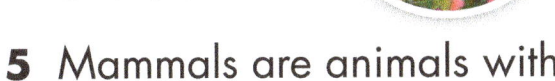

5 Mammals are animals with _____.
  a backbones
  b six legs
  c dry skin

6 A kitten is a _____.
  a baby bear
  b baby dog
  c baby cat

Body and Health

What do I need to be healthy?

1 Is this food healthy? Look and mark what is good for you (✓) and what is bad for you (✗).

1 vegetables ✓   2 sugar ☐   3 soda ☐

4 water ☐   5 meat ☐   6 fish ☐

2 What makes a healthy lunch? Think. Draw and label a healthy lunch. Use the words from the box.

| meat   vegetables   fish   fruit   milk |

3 Were you right? Read and check your answers in **1**.

Reading Tip

Read to check your ideas.

What's good for you?

Some things are good for you, and some things are bad for you. Eating vegetables, fish, and meat, and drinking water is good for you. Using soap to wash your hands is also good for you. Wearing a helmet when you are on a bicycle helps you to stay healthy and safe. But eating a lot of sugar and drinking a lot of soda is bad for you!

4 Are these things good or bad for you? Write.

1 Wearing a helmet is __good for you__.

2 Washing with soap is _____.

3 Drinking water is _____.

4 Eating a lot of sugar is _____.

5 Drinking a lot of soda is _____.

5 Draw one thing that is good for you and one thing that is bad for you. Write.

_____ _____
is good for me.   is bad for me.

Unit 4 31

Lesson 1 • What can I do to stay healthy?

1 Healthy habits. Read and match.

1 healthy — c good for you
2 a habit — a something you do again and again
3 eating well — b eating different types of healthy food

2 Look at the healthy habits. Unscramble and write.

1 agenti lewl
   eating well

2 ginexerics
   _____

3 ihwsnag dhsna
   _____

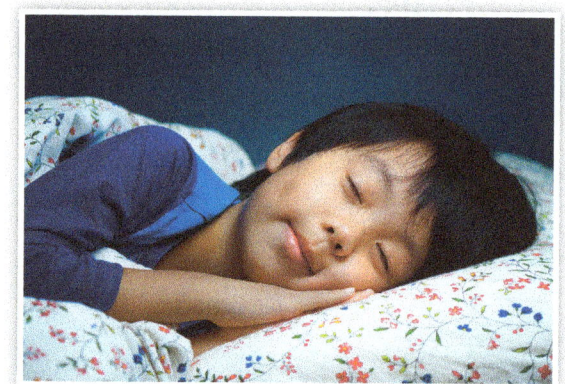

4 pesnleig
   _____

32 Unit 4

3 What is the girl doing? Write *yes* or *no*.

> **Grammar Tip**
>
> **Is** she watch**ing** TV?
> Yes, she is.
> No, she isn't.
> What **is** he do**ing**?
> Why **is** he do**ing** it?

1 Is she watching TV? ____yes____
2 Is she exercising? _____
3 Is she eating potato chips? _____
4 Is she drinking soda? _____
5 Is she sleeping? _____
6 Is she doing unhealthy things? _____

4 Your sleeping habits. Answer the questions.

Are you getting a good night's sleep?

1 Is sleep good for you?
_____

2 How many hours do you sleep each night?
_____

3 How many hours do you think you need to sleep?
_____

4 Do you think you need to sleep more?
_____

5 Is sleeping well a healthy habit or a bad habit?
_____

5 Why are they doing these things? Look, read, and match.

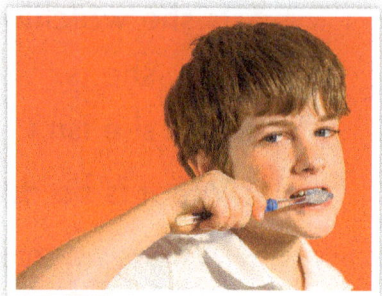

1 Why is he brushing his teeth? `d`

2 Why is he taking a shower? ☐

3 Why is she washing her hands? ☐

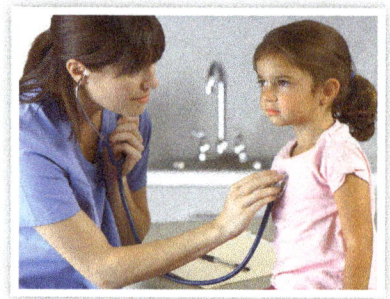

4 Why is she going to the doctor? ☐

a To get a check up.

b To get her hands clean before she eats.

c To get his body and hair clean.

d He doesn't want to get a cavity.

6 What healthy habits do you have? Complete for you.

> wear a helmet   eat well   wash hands
> go to the doctor for a check up   brush teeth to not get a cavity
> sleep well   exercise

I _____

_____

_____.

Lesson 2 · How can I stay healthy and safe?

1 Staying healthy. Look, read, and match.

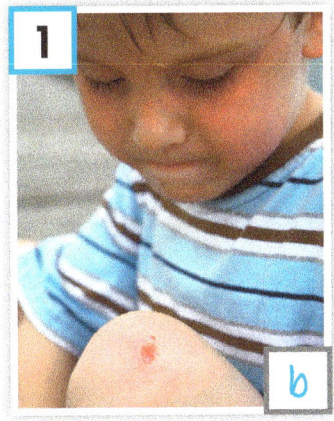

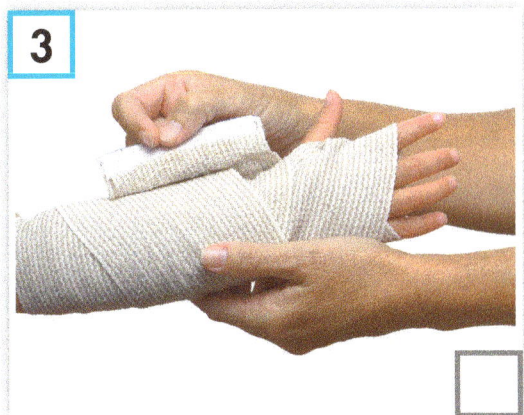

1. b
2. ☐
3. ☐

a Cover the cut with a bandage.

b You can get a cut on your skin, but your skin can heal itself.

c Wash the cut with soap and water to kill any germs.

2 Read and match.

1 You get germs
2 Germs can
3 When you sneeze,

a make you sick.
b you spread germs.
c on your hands or in a cut.

(1 — c)

3 How do you treat a cut to stop germs from making you sick? Draw and write.

1 _____
   _____
   _____

2 _____
   _____
   _____

Unit 4   35

4 How can you stay safe when you play? Look, read, and write.

helmet   street   ~~water~~   life jacket

1 Be careful near ___water.___ An adult needs to watch you when you swim.

2 Be careful near water. Wear a _____ in a boat.

3 Be careful of cars. Don't play in the _____.

4 Wear a _____ when you ride a bike.

5 Make rules for staying safe. Read and write.

~~ride your bike in the street~~
wear a life jacket in a boat
wear a helmet   play in the street

Grammar Tip

Wear a helmet when you ride a bike.
Don't play in the street.

DO	DON'T
_____	_Don't ride your bike in the street._
_____	_____

6 What do you do to stay safe? Write.

I _____ to stay safe.

36 Unit 4

7 Safety in the sun. Read and match.

1 sunburn — a You wear them when it is sunny.
2 sunscreen — b Your skin turns red and feels hot.
3 sunglasses — c This lotion keeps you safe from the sun.

8 Do the quiz about safety in the sun. Read and circle.

What do you need to do in the sun?

1 Put on sunscreen
   - (a) before you go outside.
   - b after you go outside.

2 Put on more sunscreen
   - a after you have dinner.
   - b after you go swimming.

3 Wear sunscreen on _____ not covered by clothes.
   - a your head
   - b all parts of your body

4 Wear sunglasses when
   - a it's sunny.
   - b it's cold.

9 Draw yourself at the beach in the sun. Write two things you need to do.

1 _____

2 _____

Unit 4   37

Unit 5 Earth and Sky

What can you say about Earth and sky?

1 What can you see? Look and write.

| ocean | moon | ~~sun~~ | rock | cloud | tree |

1. sun
2. _____
3. _____
4. _____
5. _____
6. _____

2 Read and circle *T* (true) or *F* (false).

1 We can find clouds in the sky. **(T)** / F
2 The moon is in the sky. T / F
3 Trees grow on Earth. T / F
4 The sun is on Earth. T / F
5 We can find oceans in the sky. T / F

3 Earth and the sky. Draw and label.

Two things we can see on Earth.

Two things we can see in the sky.

38 Unit 5

4) **Which objects are made of rock? Look and mark (✓).**

1  ✓

2

3

4

5) **An object made of rock. Think, draw, and write. Use words from the box.**

statue   bridge   building
hard   big   small

This is a _____
_____.
It's _____
_____.

Unit 5   39

Lesson 1 • What is on Earth?

1 What can we see on Earth? Look, read, and circle the words from the box.

mountains   hills   island   ~~plains~~

1 (Plains) are large flat areas of land.
2 Hills are where the land gets higher.
3 Mountains are the highest kind of land.
4 An island is land with water all around it.

2 What can you see? Look and write.

plain   ~~hill~~   mountain   island

1 __hill__   2 _____   3 _____   4 _____

3 What can you find near where you live? Mark (✓) and write.

a hill ☐   an island ☐   a plain ☐   a mountain ☐
a river ☐   a lake ☐   an ocean ☐

There is _____ near me.
There is _____ near me.
There isn't _____ near me.
There isn't _____ near me.

> **Grammar Tip**
>
> There is **a** lake.
> There is **an** ocean.

40 Unit 5

4 Think and complete the mind maps.

~~ocean~~   river   soil   rocks   lake

Land
____   ____

Water
____   ____   ocean

5 Were you right? Read and check your answers in **4**.

On Earth, there are different kinds of land and water. Land has rocks and soil. Rocks are hard, and soil is soft. Different kinds of places with water are oceans, rivers, and lakes. An ocean is a large area of salt water. Oceans cover most of Earth. A lake has land all around it. Rivers flow from the land to the ocean. Their water doesn't have any salt.

6 How are rivers and oceans different? Read and write.

flow across the land   have salt in the water

Rivers
____
____

water on Earth

Oceans
____
____

7 What do you like/don't you like on Earth? Mark (✓) and (✗). Then write.

hills ☐   islands ☐   plains ☐   mountains ☐
rivers ☐   lakes ☐   oceans ☐

I like _____. I don't like _____.

Unit 5   41

Lesson 2 · What changes land?

1 Look and write.

volcano
earthquake

_____ _____

2 How does the land change after a volcano? Read and draw.

Before
The land and trees look green.

After
The land looks dry.
The trees have disappeared.

3 Do the changes happen fast or slowly? Read and circle.

1 A river goes across the land.   fast / (slowly)

2 A volcano erupts.   fast / slowly

3 Earthquakes crack the land.   fast / slowly

4 Weathering breaks rocks with ice or water.   fast / slowly

5 Erosion, by wind or water, moves rocks.   fast / slowly

4 What changes the land? Look, unscramble, and write.

anetherigw   renoosi   queekartha

1 __weathering__   2 _____   3 _____

5 Changes on Earth. Read and circle.

Reading Tip
Read the text slowly to help you choose the best word.

(1) **Weathering** / **Volcano** is when water or ice breaks down rocks. (2) **Erosion** / **Volcano** is when wind or water moves rocks and soil. (3) **Weathering** / **Earthquake** and erosion can take a long time. They change Earth (4) **fast** / **slowly**.

6 What changes the land? Draw and label two changes.

erosion   weathering   volcano   earthquake

Unit 5 43

Lesson 3 • What is the sun?

1 **The sun. Look and match.**

a Living things need heat from the sun.

b A star is a big ball of hot gas.

c The sun lights Earth.

d The sun warms the land, the water, and the air.

2 **Why do we need the sun? Read and circle the words from the box.**

heat   live   grow   warms

We Need the Sun

When there isn't any sunlight, it is cold. The sun warms Earth. It gives us heat. We need the light from the sun to see. When there isn't any sunlight, plants cannot grow, and animals and people cannot live. We cannot live without the sun.

3 **Read 2 again and write.**

1 We need the sun to w_arm_ Earth.

2 People need the light from the sun to s_____.

3 Plants need the sun to g_____.

4 Animals need the heat from the sun to l_____.

5 People need the h_____ from the sun to live.

4 What do they use in the sun? Look and write.

1. sunscreen
2. _____
3. _____

5 What do you need to do in the sun?
Design a poster. Use the words in the box.

> **Reading Tip**
> Think about who the poster is for.

> The sun can harm you.
> Protect yourself.
> Never look at the sun!
> Wear…

6 What do you use in the sun? Draw one or two objects and complete for you.

I wear _____
_____.

Unit 6 Weather

How can you describe weather?

1 What can you see? Look and match.

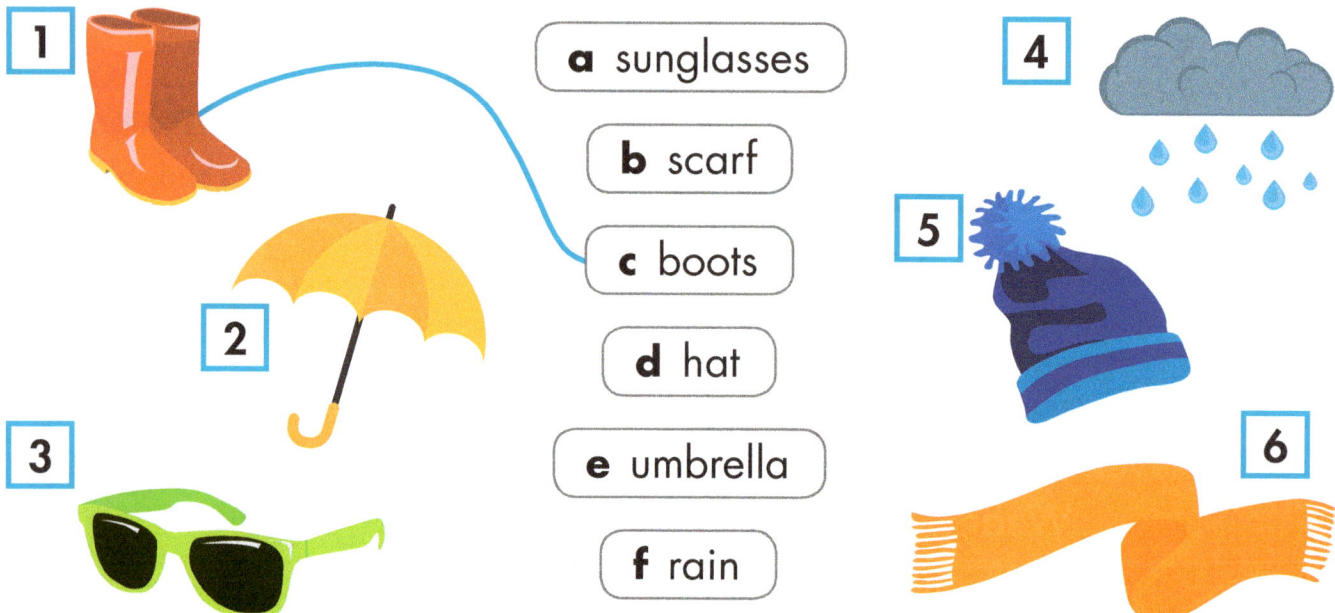

- a sunglasses
- b scarf
- c boots
- d hat
- e umbrella
- f rain

2 What do you use when the weather changes? Read and circle.

1 What do you take with you when there is rain?
   - a sunglasses
   - b scarf
   - (c) umbrella

2 What do you wear when there is snow?
   - a sunglasses
   - b hat and scarf
   - c shoes

3 What do you wear when it is sunny?
   - a boots
   - b umbrella
   - c sunglasses

4 What is difficult to use when there is a lot of wind?
   - a umbrella
   - b scarf
   - c boots

3 Read the title of the text in **4**. Mark (✓) the words you expect to find.

sun ✓   snow ☐   cloud ☐
moon ☐   water ☐   island ☐   rain ☐   grass ☐

Reading Tip

Think about the text before you read it.

4 Read and circle *T* (true) or *F* (false).

Where does rain come from?

Heat from the sun warms the land and the water. Some of the water in the oceans, lakes, and rivers goes up into the air as gas. The gas cools and makes clouds. The clouds can make rain, and the rain falls back down to the land.

1 Heat warms the land. **T** / F
2 Water goes down into the air. T / F
3 The gas warms. T / F
4 The gas cools and makes clouds. T / F
5 The clouds can make rain. T / F
6 The rain falls back to the land. T / F

5 Draw you on a rainy day. Label the objects. Complete the sentences.

I'm wearing _____ because it's a rainy day.
I _____
_____
_____.

Unit 6   47

Lesson 1 • What is weather?

1 What's the weather like? Look and match.

a hurricane   b snowstorm   c thunderstorm   d tornado

2 What can you remember? Read and match.

1 Weather is   a rain, lightning, and thunder.
2 A storm is a kind of   b a very bad storm.
3 A thunderstorm has   c what it is like outside.
4 A tornado has   d lots of snow.
5 A hurricane is   e very strong winds.
6 Snowstorms can bring   f bad weather.

3 Look, circle, and write.

1 _____   2 _____
3 _____   4 _____
5 _____   6 _____

weather • storm • snowstorm • hurricane • tornado • thunderstorm

48 Unit 6

4 Read the title of the text in **5**. Mark (✓) the words you expect to find.

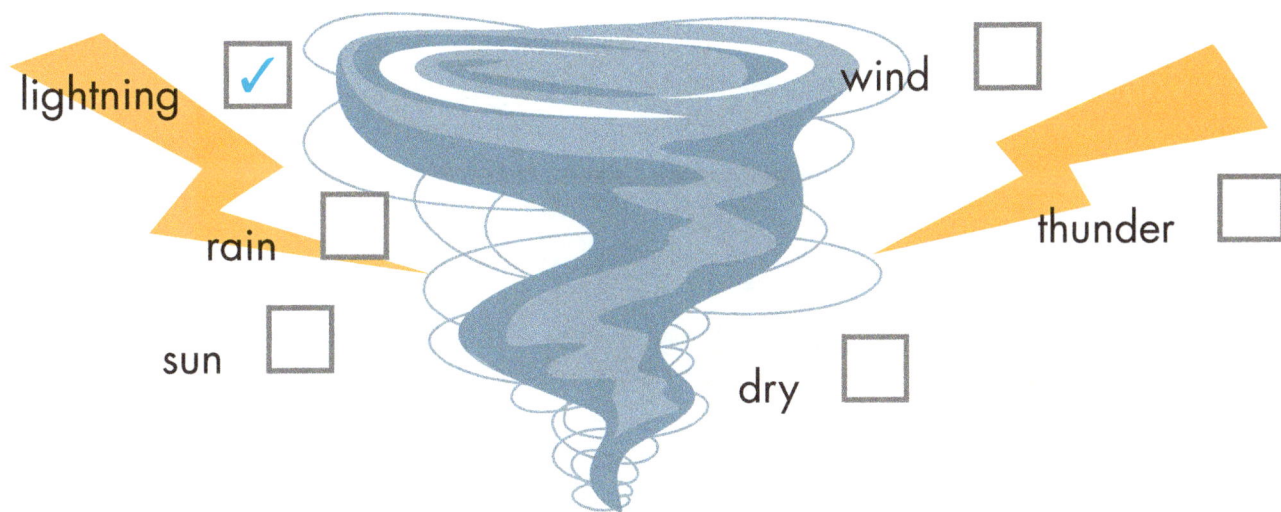

lightning ✓ wind ☐ rain ☐ thunder ☐ sun ☐ dry ☐

5 Read and write *yes* or *no*.

Tornadoes

A tornado can happen during a thunderstorm, with lightning, rain, and thunder. Tornadoes have very strong winds. They move very fast. You need to find shelter in a basement, or in a place with no windows.

1 Can a tornado happen during a thunderstorm? ____yes____

2 Is there snow in a tornado? _____

3 Are there strong winds? _____

4 Is it a good idea to find shelter near a window? _____

6 How do you keep safe in bad weather? Complete for you.

I take shelter in _____.

I go to a _____.

Unit 6   49

Lesson 2 · How can you measure weather?

1 What can you see? Look and write.

wind vane   ~~thermometer~~   rain gauge

1. thermometer
2. _____
3. _____

2 How can you measure the weather? Read and write.

thermometer   rain gauge   wind vane   ~~measure~~   temperature

You can use different tools to **(1)** m_easure_ rainy weather, windy weather, and the **(2)** t_____. The **(3)** r_____ measures how much rain has fallen. The **(4)** w_____ shows the direction of the wind. The **(5)** t_____ measures the temperature—how hot or cold it is.

3 What's the weather like? Read and draw the weather tools.

This is my weather station. I have a **rain gauge** to measure the rain. There isn't any rain in it today.

I have a **wind vane** to show the wind direction. The wind is coming from the west.

I also have a **thermometer** to measure the temperature. Today it's 22 °C. It's warm.

4 **Read 3 again and circle.**

1 I has / (have) three measuring tools.

2 There is / There isn't any rain in it today.

3 The wind / rain is coming from the west.

4 It's cold / warm.

Reading Tip

Read instructions carefully, so that you know what to do.

5 **How can you measure the weather? Read and write.**

1 You can measure the weather with different _____tools_____.

2 You can see the wind direction with a _____.

3 You can measure rainy weather with _____.

4 You can measure the temperature with _____.

6 **Design and label your own weather station.**

Tools
rain gauge: rain   wind vane: wind
thermometer: temperature

Type of Weather
rainy   windy
hot   cold   warm

Unit 6 51

Lesson 3 · What are the four seasons?

1 What can you see? Match the seasons and pictures.

a fall   **b** spring   **c** winter   **d** summer

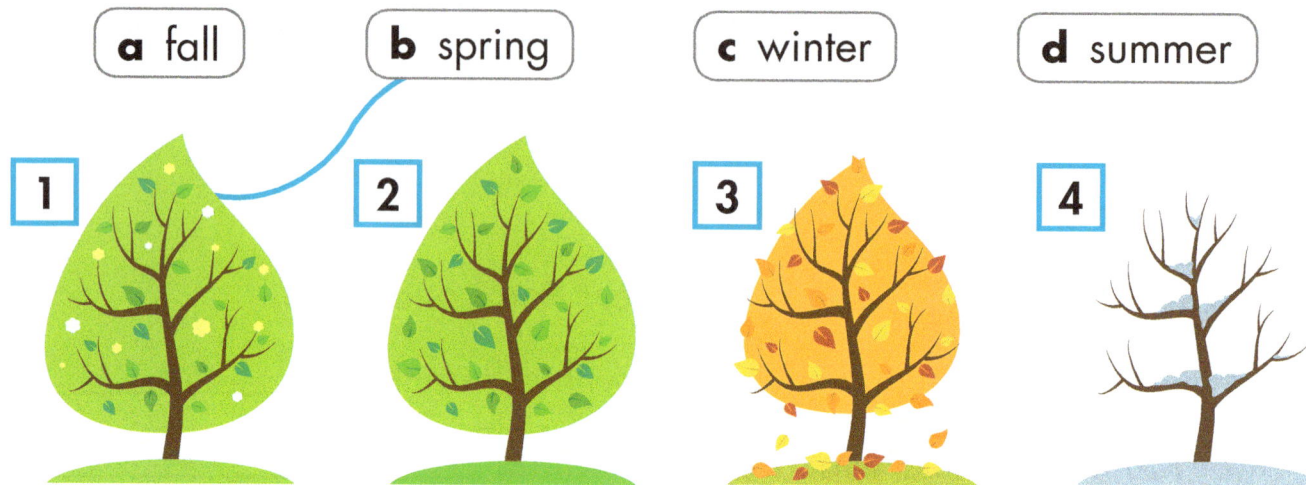

2 What happens in each season? Read and complete the chart.

spring   summer   ~~fall~~   winter

🟢🟢🟡🟤 Seasons

Spring comes before summer and after winter. It's warmer than winter, and it can rain. Summer comes before fall and after spring. It's warmer than spring, and many plants grow. Fall comes before winter and after summer. It's cooler than summer. Some leaves change colors. Winter comes before spring and after fall. It can be the coldest season. It can snow in some places.

Season	Temperature	What Can Happen
1 fall	cooler than summer	leaves change colors
2	warmer than winter	it can rain
3	the coldest season	it can snow
4	warmer than spring	plants grow

3 What's your favorite season? Complete for you. Use the words in the box.

Grammar Tip
Spring comes **before** summer.
Spring comes **after** winter.

| hot | dry | wet | warm |
| green | plants | snow | leaves |

1 My favorite season is _____.

2 I like it because it's _____.

4 When are the seasons? Look and complete.

5 Look at **4**. Read and complete with *before* or *after*.

1 Spring comes ___after___ winter and ___before___ summer.

2 Summer comes _____ fall and _____ spring.

3 Fall comes _____ winter and _____ summer.

4 Winter comes _____ fall and _____ spring.

6 What do you do in each season? Complete for you.

In spring, I like to _____.

In summer, _____.

In fall, _____.

In winter, _____.

Review 4-6

1. Can you remember these words about health? Look, circle, and write.

1 _____
2 _____
3 _____
4 _____
5 _____
6 _____
7 _____
8 _____
9 _____

2. Which is the odd word out? Read and circle.

1 exercise   healthy   sick   germs   (plain)
2 hill   island   sunglasses   mountain   lake
3 erosion   rain gauge   wind vane   tool   thermometer
4 star   sky   Earth   earthquake   sun
5 thunderstorm   storm   tornado   hurricane   scarf
6 habit   cavity   check up   weathering   skin
7 fall   snowstorm   spring   winter   summer
8 warm   heat   sun   volcano

3 What's the season? Read, think, and write.

I come before winter.
I come after summer.
Leaves change colors.
What season am I?

_____

4 Complete the crossword.

```
 1P
 2l    3    4  5
  a
  i                    6
7 i
  n    8
```

Across →

2 Water that has land all around it.

4 Land with water all around.

7 Water that goes across land.

8 It measures temperature.

Down ↓

1 A large, flat area of land.

3 It has land and water, and air all around it.

5 A big ball of hot gas.

6 The sun does this to the land, the water, and the air.

Unit 7 Matter

How can you describe matter?

1) **What can you see? Look and match.**

2) **What are the objects made of? Look at 1 again. Read and write.**

~~plastic~~   water   plastic   air   plastic   liquid soap

1 The bottle of water is made of __plastic.__
2 The jar is made of _____.
3 The bubble is made of _____, _____, and _____.
4 The bubble wand is made of _____.

3) **What have you got at home to make bubbles? Read and mark (✓).**

water ☐
plastic jar ☐
liquid soap ☐
bubble wand ☐

56 Unit 7

4 How do you make bubbles? Look, read, and match.

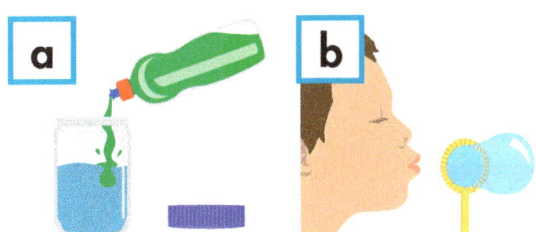

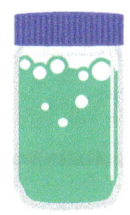

How to make bubbles
You need:
3 cups of water
1 cup of liquid soap
a plastic jar
a bubble wand

1 Collect the things you need. — c
2 Mix the water and the liquid soap in a plastic jar. ☐
3 Leave for a few hours. ☐
4 Make bubbles with the bubble wand. ☐

5 Now you can make some bubbles. Draw, color, and write.

red   green   blue   water   yellow
air   big   small   liquid soap

The bubbles are made of _____.
They are _____. (size)
They are _____. (color)

Unit 7   57

Lesson 1 · What is matter?

1 Matter or mass? Read and circle *matter* and *mass*.

What is (matter)?

Matter is everything around us. Matter is anything that has mass and takes up space.

What is mass?

Mass is the amount of matter in an object.

2 What can you remember? Read and match.

1 weight
2 float
3 sink
4 length

a how long an object is
b to fall to the bottom of a liquid
c how heavy an object is
d to stay on top of a liquid

(1 weight — c how heavy an object is)

3 What do you know about these objects? Complete the chart.

toy boat   beach ball   nails   rock   ice cream   ice cubes

1 Two things that float	
2 Two things that sink	
3 Two things made out of plastic	
4 Two things that are cold	ice cubes

58 Unit 7

4 Light or heavy? Order the objects from light to heavy (1–3).

tennis ball ☐   soccer ball ☐   marble ☐

5 What does this child's bedroom look like? Read and draw.

> **My Bedroom**
> There is a big, round clock on the wall. There are three small, hard, green marbles on the table. There is a big, soft, blue ball on the chair. There is a long, soft, red scarf on the bed. There are three small, round, yellow lights.

> **Grammar Tip**
> There is a **long**, **soft**, **red** scarf on the bed.

6 What does your bedroom look like? Complete for you.

hard	soft	red	blue	green	heavy
long	bed	table	green	clock	

1 There is a _____ in my bedroom.

2 There is a _____.

3 There is a _____.

Unit 7 59

Lesson 2 · What are solids, liquids, and gases?

1 Which of these objects are solids? Look and circle.

(ice cubes)   water   table   apple   rain

> A solid object has its own shape. It does not change size and shape when you move it.

2 Solid, liquid, or gas? Read and complete the mind maps.

rock   milk   air   juice   chair
soda pop   sky   an orange

3 Read and circle *T* (true) or *F* (false).

1 Milk is a liquid. It takes the shape of its container.   (T) / F
2 A rock is a solid. It has its own shape.   T / F
3 Air is a gas. It can change shape.   T / F
4 A chair is a solid. It is often invisible.   T / F

4 What can you remember? Read and match.

1 Freeze — a means to heat a liquid until it changes into a gas.
2 Melt — b means to change from a liquid to a solid.
3 Boil   c means to change from a solid to a liquid.

5 How can matter change? Read the text and complete the graph.

Reading Tip
A graph shows information in a way that makes it easy to understand.

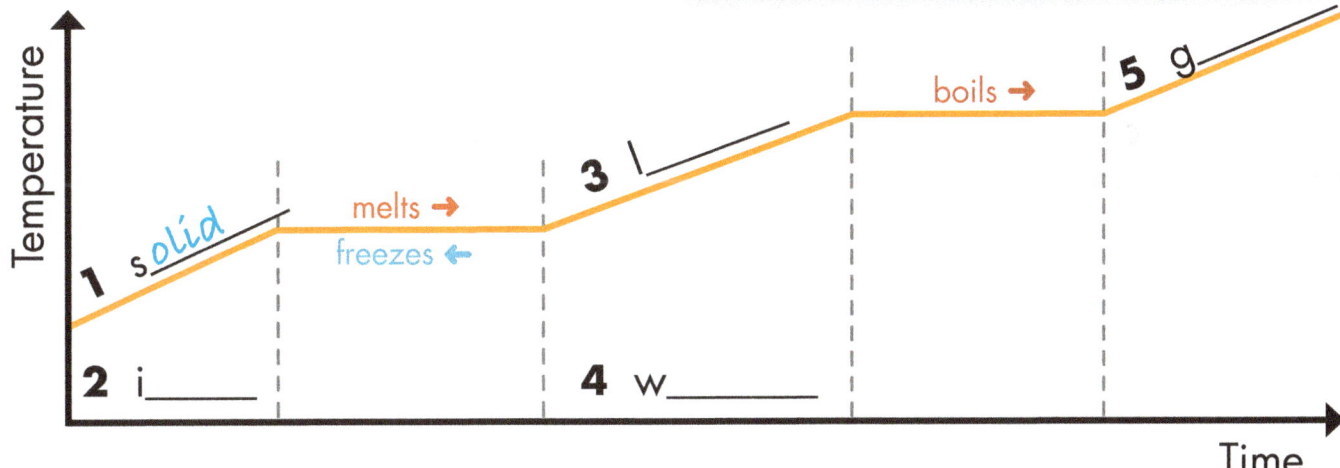

1 s.olid
2 i_____
3 l_____
4 w_____
5 g_____

How Matter Changes

Ice is a solid. When it gets warm, ice melts. It changes into water. Water is a liquid. Water freezes when it gets very cold. It changes into ice. Water can evaporate when it boils. Then it becomes a gas.

6 What matter can you see at home? Think and write the name of a solid, a liquid, and a gas.

A solid: _____
A liquid: _____
A gas: _____

Lesson 3 · How can matter change?

1 How can matter change? Look and mark (✓) the changes.

	Cook Popcorn	Bend a Straw	Cut Paper
Shape	✓		
Size			
Color			

2 How can matter change? Choose an object from 1. Write and draw.

1 Write the name of the object. _____

2 Draw pictures to show what it looks like before and after the change.

Before	After

3 Describe the change. Use the words from 1.

_____ can change. You can _____ it.

It changes _____. It doesn't change _____.

62 Unit 7

3 How can these materials change? Read and write.

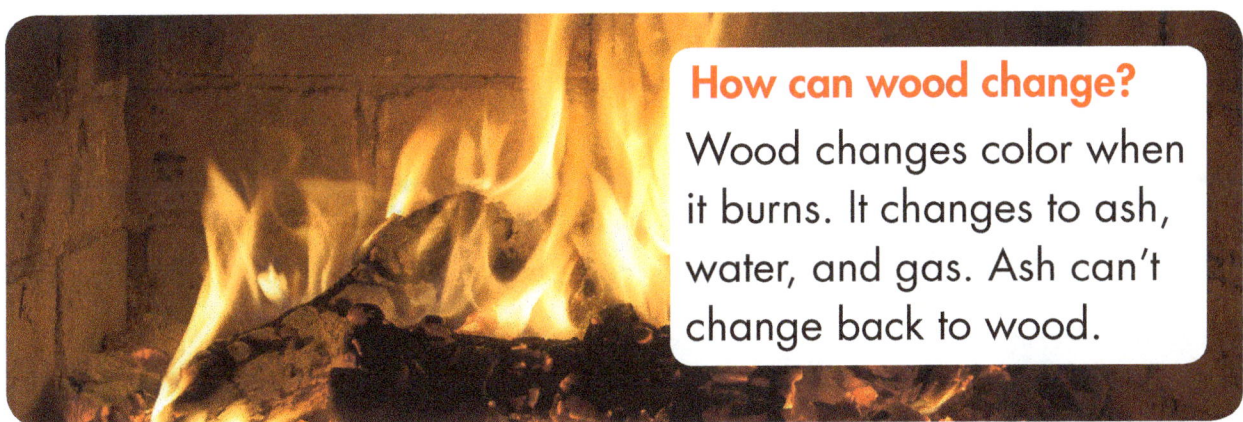

How can wood change?
Wood changes color when it burns. It changes to ash, water, and gas. Ash can't change back to wood.

How can iron change?
Iron can turn into rust when it gets wet. Iron and oxygen make up rust. Rust can't change back to iron.

1 Wood can change to gas, water, and a_____.

2 Iron can turn into r_____. I_____ and o_____ make up rust.

4 Read and complete the sentences with *can* or *can't*.

1 Iron ___can___ turn into rust.

2 Water _____ turn into ice.

3 Ice _____ turn into water.

4 Water _____ turn into gas.

5 Ash _____ change back to wood.

Grammar Tip

Wood **can** burn.
Rust **can't** change back.

Unit 7 63

Unit 8 Energy

What can energy do?

1 Energy in our lives. Circle in red the things that give us energy. Circle in blue the things that use energy.

2 Do they give energy or use energy? Read and circle.

1 The sun **gives** / **uses** energy.
2 The electric fan **gives** / **uses** energy.
3 The iron **gives** / **uses** energy.
4 The oil **gives** / **uses** energy.
5 The plane **gives** / **uses** energy.
6 The coal **gives** / **uses** energy.

3 What gives energy? Draw and write. Choose from the words in the box.

| gives | the sun | coals |
| give | oil | gas |

_____ energy.

4 What do they give energy to? Look and match.

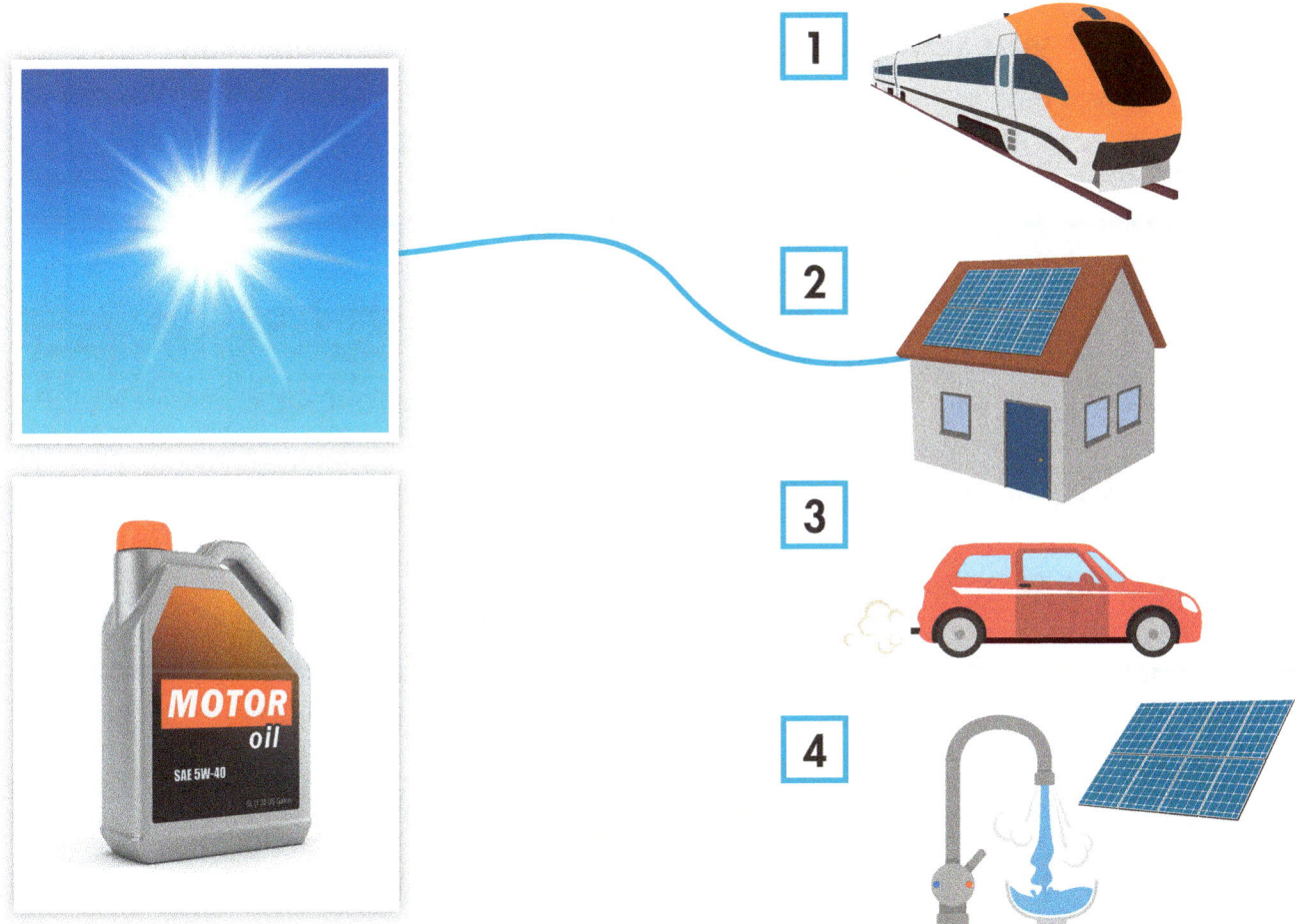

5 Were you right? Read and check your answers in 4.

The sun can give energy to homes. It can make the house and the water hot. Oil can give energy to trains and cars.

6 What uses energy in your home? Think and complete for you.

1 _____ uses energy in my home.

2 _____

3 _____

Unit 8 65

Lesson 1 · How do we use energy?

1 What can you see? Mark (✓) the things that use electricity.

streetlight ✓
car ☐
light in a home ☐
backpack ☐
umbrella ☐

2 How does a bus move? Read and write.

engine   fuel   ~~use~~   gasoline   energy

Buses (1) __use__ energy. Most buses get energy from (2) _____. The fuel burns to make heat or power. Buses use (3) _____ for fuel. A bus (4) _____ burns the gasoline. The bus has (5) _____ to move.

3 Read and circle T (true) or F (false). Use the text in 2 to help you.

1 Buses don't use energy.   T /(F)
2 Buses get energy from fuel.   T / F
3 Fuel burns to make heat or power.   T / F
4 Buses use water for fuel.   T / F
5 The engine in the bus burns the fuel. T / F

4 What can you remember? Read and match.

Grammar Tip

What do batteries **do**?
Batteries **store** energy.
Batteries **change** the stored energy into electricity.

1 The toy car — a energy.
2 The toy car uses   b the stored energy into electricity.
3 Batteries store   c electricity to move.
4 Batteries change   d needs energy to move.

5 What are the actions? Read the Grammar Tip and underline the verbs.

6 Draw one toy that gets energy from batteries. Draw one toy that uses a key. Write.

| toy train | toy bus | doll | toy car |
| robot | teddy bear |

1 The _____ gets energy from _____.

2 The _____ uses a _____.

Unit 8   67

Lesson 2 · What is light?

1 Which things does light come from? Look and mark (✓).

2 Read and circle the objects that make a shadow.

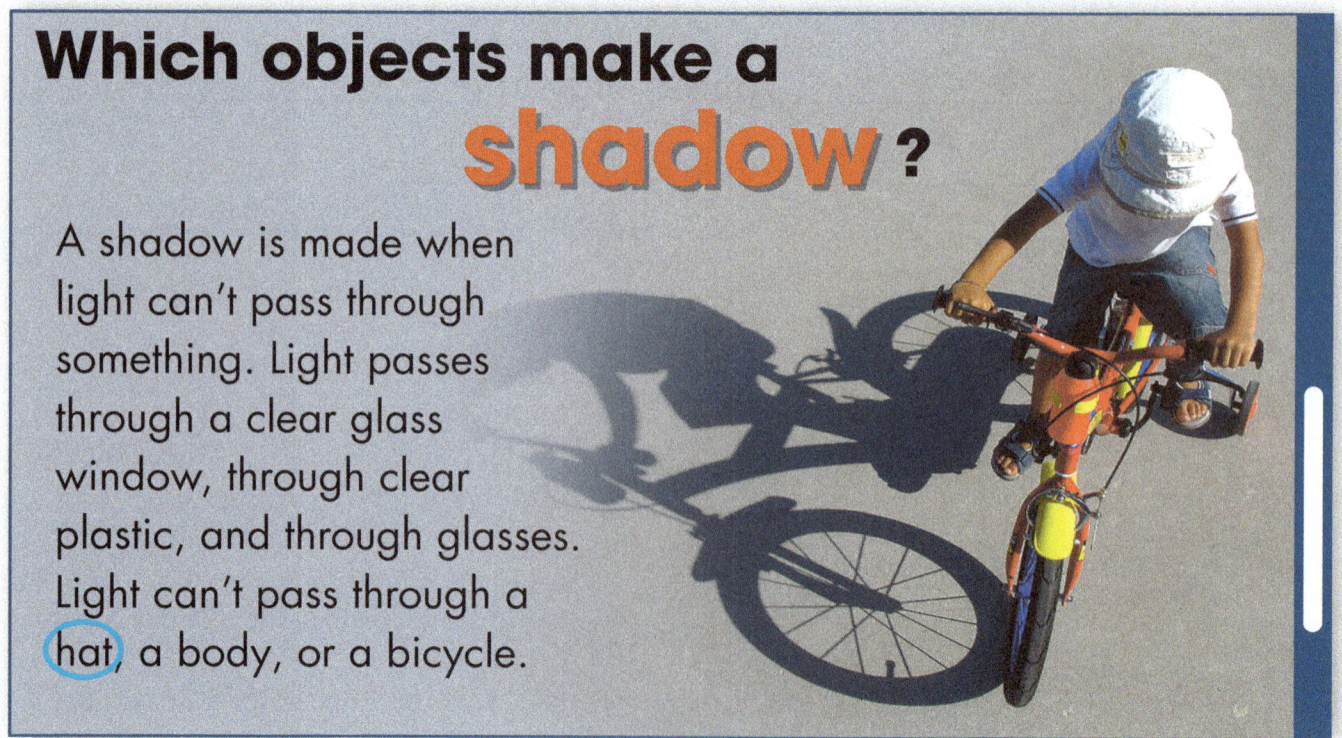

Which objects make a shadow?

A shadow is made when light can't pass through something. Light passes through a clear glass window, through clear plastic, and through glasses. Light can't pass through a (hat), a body, or a bicycle.

3 What can light do? Look and read. Write *yes* or *no*.

Grammar Tip

Light bounces **back** to you from a mirror.
Light passes **through** glass.
Light bounces **off** smooth and shiny objects.

1 Does light pass through a clear glass window? __yes__

2 Does light bounce off shiny marbles? _____

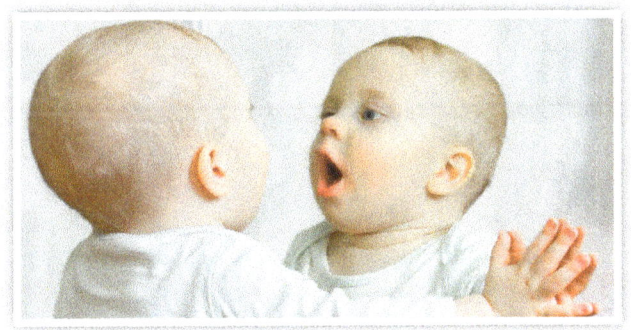

3 Does light bounce back to you from a mirror? _____

4 Does light pass through a bicycle? _____

4 Which objects does light pass through? Write about three objects.

| a window | a chair | thin paper | a rabbit |
| sunglasses | a clear plastic bag | a door |

1 Light passes through _____.

2 _____

3 _____

Unit 8   **69**

Lesson 3 • What is sound?

1 Which object makes both light and sound? Look and circle.

1

2

3

4

2 How do we hear the guitar? Read and order the sentences.

a We hear the sounds. ☐

b A boy plucks the guitar strings. 1

c The strings vibrate. ☐

3 What's your favorite instrument? Think, write, and circle.

> guitar   drums   recorder   piano

My favorite instrument is the _____.

I **can** / **can't** play it.

70 Unit 8

4 What kind of sound can they make? Look and write *soft* or *loud*.

1
loud

2
_____

3
_____

4
_____

5 High or low? Read and answer the questions.

Some animal sounds are high. Other animal sounds are low. I can hear a cow. It makes a low sound. I can hear a cat. It makes a high sound. I can hear a baby bird. It makes a high sound. Small animals often make high sounds. Big animals often make low sounds.

1 Is the sound of a cow low?   _Yes, it is._

2 Is the sound of a cat low?   _____

3 Is the sound of a bird high? _____

Reading Tip

Read a text before you read the questions. Then read the text again.

6 What sound do you like? What sound don't you like? Complete for you.

| high   low   loud   soft |

1 I like the sound of _____. It makes a _____ sound.

2 I don't like the sound of _____. It makes a _____ sound.

Unit 8

Unit 9 Movement

How can you describe ways objects move?

1 What makes the objects move? Look and write.

water
air
~~hand~~

1 The _hand_ pushes the car. It is moving the toy car.

2 The _____ is moving the plastic duck.

3 The girl blows the plant. The _____ is moving the plant.

2 Can you move the objects easily? Look and write *yes* or *no*.

1 __no__   2 _____   3 _____   4 _____

3 Draw two objects you can move easily. Complete for you.

1 I can move _____ easily.

2 I can _____ _____.

4 Which four things can't you move easily? Read and circle.

Reading Tip
Read the whole text to find the answer.

What can't you move?

You can move some things easily. You can move blocks, a teddy bear, a toy train, or a toy car. They all move easily. You can move a balloon and ball easily.

But you can't move some objects. (Heavy objects) can be difficult to move. This is because the force of gravity pulls them toward Earth. Big objects can be difficult to move. You can't move your house or your school.

5 Read 4 again and circle.

1 You (can) / can't move a teddy bear easily.
2 You can / can't move a ball easily.
3 You can / can't move heavy objects easily.
4 You can / can't move big objects easily.

6 Draw an object that you can't move easily. Complete for you.

big table   big chair   heavy plant

I can't move a _____.

Unit 9

Lesson 1 · How can objects move?

1 How do they move? Look and match.

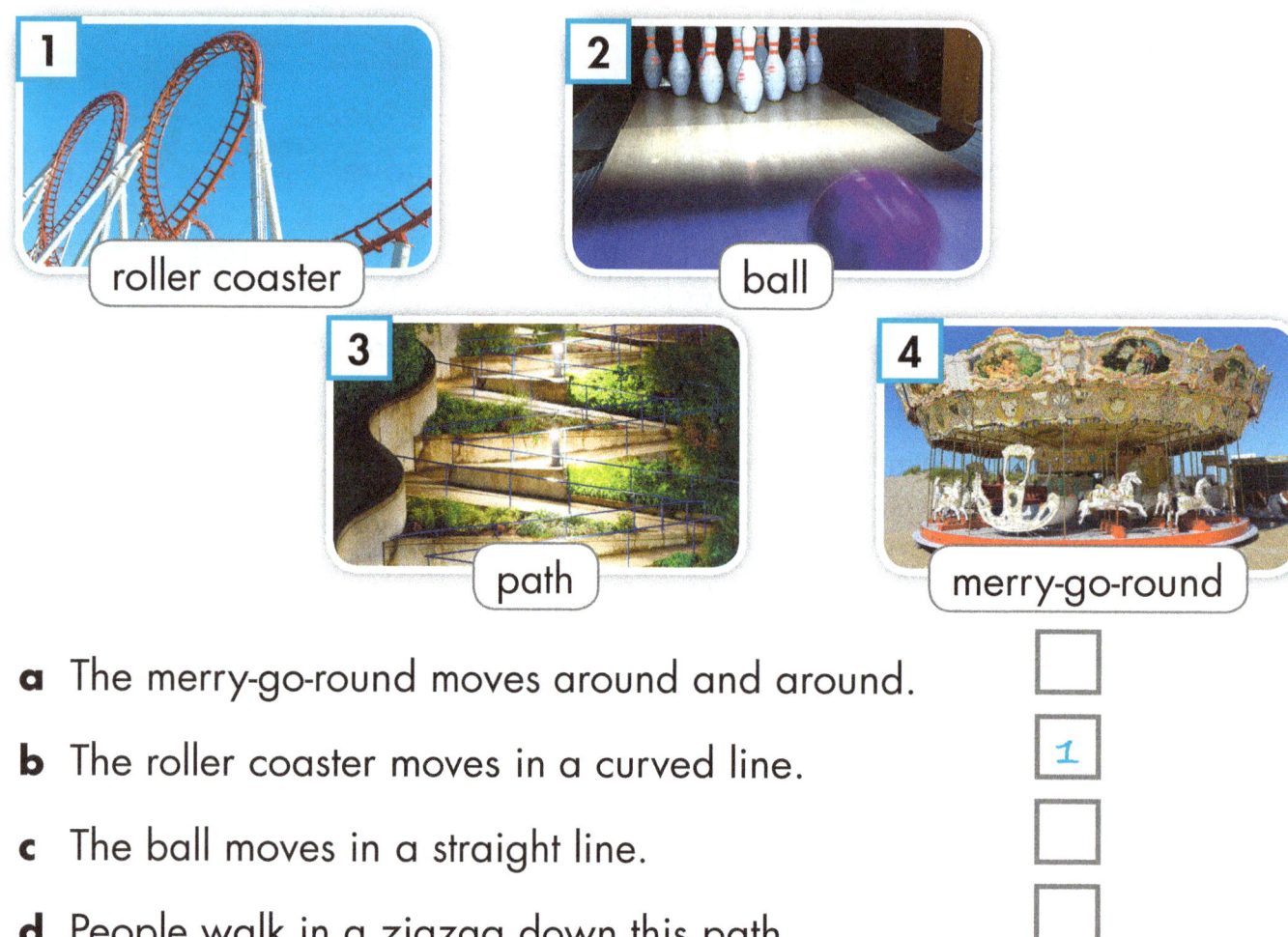

1 roller coaster
2 ball
3 path
4 merry-go-round

a The merry-go-round moves around and around. ☐

b The roller coaster moves in a curved line. [1]

c The ball moves in a straight line. ☐

d People walk in a zigzag down this path. ☐

2 What do these lines look like? Draw and write.

straight   zigzag   curved

1 This is a _____ line.

2 This is a _____ _____.

3 This is _____ _____.

74 Unit 9

3 What speed? Look and write *slowly* or *quickly*.

1 The ball is moving ___quickly___.

2 She is moving _____.

3 It is moving _____.

4 He is moving _____.

4 Read and complete the chart.

Reading Tip

Read then write in a chart.

Slowly or quickly?

Some objects and people move slowly. Some move quickly. A bubble moves slowly, but a train moves quickly. A baby moves slowly, but a child moves quickly.

Object	Speed
bubble	1 It moves slowly.
train	2
baby	3
child	4

5 How do things move at home or in the street? Read and write.

~~slowly~~   quickly   in a straight line
in a curved line   in a zigzag   around and around

1 The clock moves _____slowly_____.

2 _____ moves quickly.

3 _____ moves _____.

Unit 9   75

Lesson 2 • What is a force?

1 What can you see in the pictures? Write *push* or *pull*.

1 ___push___

2 _____

3 _____

4 _____

2 Read and circle *T* (true) or *F* (false).

PUSH or PULL?

A push and a pull are forces. You can pull a door to open it. You can push a door to close it. You can push a marble or a ball. You can pull a drawer to open it, and you can push a drawer to shut it. Don't push or pull big or heavy objects. Ask an adult to help you.

1 A push and a pull are forces.   **T** / F

2 You can pull a door to open it.   T / F

3 Push a drawer to open it.   T / F

4 Push a drawer to close it.   T / F

5 Ask an adult to help you move heavy objects.   T / F

3 What can a force do? Look and write.

1 A force can ___start___ an object moving.

2 A force can _____ the direction of an object.

3 A force can _____ a moving object.

change
~~start~~
stop

4 Read and circle six words you know.

Reading Tip
Find words you know.

CHANGING MOTION

The mother changes the motion of the swing less when she pushes it with less force. The boy changes the motion of the bike more when he pushes his feet down with more force.

5 What is motion? Read and match.

1 Motion is   a and the motion of an object changes more.

2 Use more force,   b and the motion of an object changes less.

3 Use less force,   c the act of moving.

Lesson 3 · What is gravity?

1 **What is gravity? Read and match.**

a   Gravity keeps the boy on the ground.

b   Gravity pulls the ball down toward Earth.

2 **What keeps the kite in the air? Read and write.**

gravity   ~~kite~~   wind   string

The girl loves flying her
(1) ___kite___. (2) _____ pulls down on the kite. The (3) _____ holds up the kite. Gravity pulls down on the roll of string. The girl holds up the roll of (4) _____.

3 **What happens when the wind stops holding up the kite? Circle and draw.**

Gravity pulls the kite **up** / **down**.

78   Unit 9

4 Read and circle *T* (true) or *F* (false).

1 Gravity can't pull objects without touching them.   T / **F**

2 The water comes out of the fountain quickly.   T / F

3 Something holds the water up.   T / F

4 Gravity pulls the water down without touching it.   T / F

Water Coming Up and Down

Look at the fountain in the park. The water shoots out, but nothing holds it up. How does the water come down? Gravity pulls it down, but it doesn't touch it.

5 Read and write *up* or *down*.

1 Gravity pulls objects _down_ toward Earth.

2 The water comes _____ out of the fountain.

3 Nothing holds the water _____.

4 Gravity pulls the water _____.

6 What can you hold up? Complete for you and draw.

1 I hold up the ___balloon___.

2 I hold up _____ _____.

~~balloon~~   ball
umbrella   toy car
teddy bear

Review 7-9

1 What's the opposite? Look, unscramble, and write.

   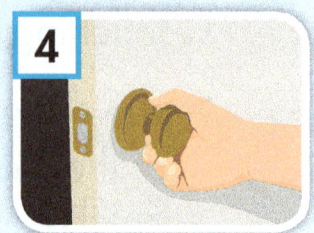

1 opposite of melt [ezfere] = f<u>reeze</u>

2 opposite of slowly [lqicyku] = q_____

3 opposite of pull [shup] = p_____

4 opposite of push [lplu] = p_____

2 What are they? Read and answer the question.

We move in the air.
We float on water.
You can make us from liquid soap.
What are we?

_____

3 Which is the odd word out? Read and circle.

1 bubbles   liquid soap   bubble wand   water   (ash)

2 electricity   shadow   energy   fuel   battery

3 gravity   move   straight   curved   around

4 sound   vibrate   loud   iron   high

5 matter   mass   weight   float   engine

4 What can you remember? Do the quiz. Circle a, b, or c.

1 Weight is _____.
   (a) how heavy an object is
   b how big an object is
   c how small an object is

2 Float is _____.
   a to stay at the bottom of a liquid
   b to fall to the bottom of a liquid
   c to stay on the top of a liquid

3 Freeze means to change _____.
   a from a liquid to a gas
   b from a liquid to a solid
   c from a solid to a liquid

4 Sound is a kind of _____.
   a energy
   b fuel
   c gasoline

5 Speed is _____.
   a how quickly an object moves
   b how slowly an object moves
   c how quickly or slowly an object moves

6 A force is _____.
   a the direction of a moving object
   b a push or a pull
   c the act of moving

Vocabulary

Units 1–9 · What do I know?

Do you know these words? Think and trace.

Unit 1
science   computer   scientist

Unit 2
water   environment   light

Unit 3
parents   babies   young

Unit 4
healthy   exercise   doctor

Unit 5
earthquake   mountain   island

Unit 6
weather   temperature   thermometer

Unit 7
solid   liquid   oxygen

Unit 8
electricity   battery   energy

Unit 9
move   quickly   gravity

Units 1–9 · What do I know?

I can talk about…

			✓	✗
Unit 1		the design process	☐	☐
Unit 2		living things and their environments	☐	☐
Unit 3		plants and animals	☐	☐
Unit 4		my body and health	☐	☐
Unit 5		Earth and sky	☐	☐
Unit 6		weather	☐	☐
Unit 7		matter	☐	☐
Unit 8		energy	☐	☐
Unit 9		movement	☐	☐

Vocabulary 83

Reading Skills

Units 1–4 · What do I know?

Unit 1   I can read and understand a list.

> You need:
> a hammer
> some nails
> some scissors

Do you need scissors?   **Yes / No**

Unit 2   I can read and understand a fact file.

Do cows drink water? **Yes / No**

Unit 3   I can read and understand information in a simple chart.

	Backbone
Mammals	✓
Insects	✗

Do insects have a backbone? **Yes / No**

Unit 4   I can read and answer true or false questions.

Exercise is good for you.   **T / F**

Units 5–9 • What do I know?

Unit 5 I can read and understand a diagram.

Rivers   Oceans

water on Earth

Rivers and oceans are both water on Earth. **T** / **F**

Unit 6 I can choose a name for a group of words.

Read and circle the best name for the group.

spring   summer   fall   winter

weather   seasons   time

Unit 7 I can read to find the meaning of a new word.

Freeze means *to change from a liquid to a solid.*

Does water freeze when it changes to ice?   **Yes** / **No**

Unit 8 I can read to find answers to questions.

Why does a shadow form?

A shadow forms when something blocks _____.

Unit 9 I can use a picture to help me understand a concept.

Look and circle.

CHANGING MOTION

The **mother** / **child** changes the motion of the swing less when she pushes it with less force.

Reading Skills 85

Writing Skills

Units 1–4 • What do I know?

Unit 1 I can complete a sentence with a word. ☐

What is the cup made of?
The cup is made of _____.

Unit 2 I can write numbers. ☐

A heron is a bird with a long neck and _____ long, thin legs.

Unit 3 I can complete a sentence using words from a box. ☐

| feathers | ~~backbone~~ | wings |

Birds have a _backbone_, _____, and two _____.

Unit 4 I can look at a picture and complete a sentence. ☐

When you go to the beach, you need to wear _____, a hat, and use some _____.

86 Writing Skills

Units 5–9 • What do I know?

Unit 5   **I can label pictures with words.**

Label the island and the mountain.

1. _____
2. _____

Unit 6   **I can describe a season.**

| hot   wet   cold   dry   warm |

My favorite season is summer. It is _____ and _____.

Unit 7   **I can order objects from small to big.**

Write *1, 2, 3* to order the balls from small to big.

Unit 8   **I can look and find the correct information.**

| battery   key   fuel |

How does the robot move?

Wind the _____, and the toy robot moves.

Unit 9   **I can choose a sentence to label a picture.**

a Push a swing to start the swing moving.

b Push a toy to start the toy moving.

Writing Skills   **87**

Study Skills

Learning science words
- Write new words in your notebook.
- Make sure you spell the words correctly.
- Learn the words. Try to use them as much as you can.

Asking questions
- Think of a question or problem you want to find a solution for.
- Ask yourself: *Why…? What…? When…? How…?*
- Think how science can help you answer your questions.

Finding Out
- Think about how you will investigate and record what you find out.
- Do a simple experiment with your class or at home.
- Record your information in your notebook or on a computer.
- Draw a picture, take a photo, or complete a chart to show your information.

Sharing Your Results
- Share your results with your classmates.
- Show your picture, photo, or chart. Write or say your results.
- Think how you can use technology to share results.